# MORE MR. SMALL

# MORE
# MR. SMALL

## THE LITTLE AUTO
## THE LITTLE SAILBOAT
## THE LITTLE AIRPLANE

by
# LOIS LENSKI

HENRY Z. WALCK, INC.
A division of David McKay Company, Inc.
New York

# The
# LITTLE AUTO
## *By* LOIS LENSKI

*New-York*

E         Lenski, Lois
           The little auto.  Walck, 1934
           unp.  illus.

           Mr. Small has a little red auto.
        The story and pictures show Mr. Small
        taking care of his little auto.

        1. Automobiles - Fiction  I. Title

The Little Auto

Mr. Small has a little Auto. It is red and shiny. He likes to look at it.

Mr. Small keeps
the little Auto in
the garage at the
end of the
                driveway.

Mr. Small has overalls on. He is oiling the little Auto

The little Auto has
rubber tires. Mr.
Small is pumping
them up.

The little Auto
has a radiator.
Mr. Small is fill-
ing it with water.

It is a fine day.
Mr. Small is going
for a drive. He steps
on the starter.
The engine begins
to hum.

The little Auto backs
out of the garage.
It goes chug-chug
down the
                driveway.

The little Auto goes
down the road. Mr.
Small toots the horn,
"Beep, beep!" He
scares the ducks
and chickens.

A small dog follows
the little Auto,
but is soon left
far behind.

The little Auto
is going fast.  It
passes a horse
and buggy.

The little Auto
goes
UP HILL

and
the little Auto
goes DOWN
HILL!

The little Auto
comes to town.
Mr. Small drives
down the right
side of the street.

The little Auto
comes to a STOP-GO
sign, and waits for
the policeman to
turn it.

The little Auto
goes down
     MAIN STREET.

The little Auto
stops at a Filling
Station. Mr. Small
buys five gallons
of gas.

The little Auto
catches up with a
Trolley Car.     It
waits for the peo-
ple to get off.

Mr. Small parks
the little Auto in
front of a store.
He is going in to
buy a newspaper.

The little Auto
starts for home.
It comes to a red
light and waits
for it to turn
green.

On the way home
it begins to rain.
Mr. Small has to
put the top up so
he won't get wet.

"Pop!"
Mr. Small has a
flat tire'

Mr. Small jacks the little Auto up. He puts on the spare tire.  And then the sun comes out!

Soon the little Auto is back in the garage. After it is washed and polished it shines like new.

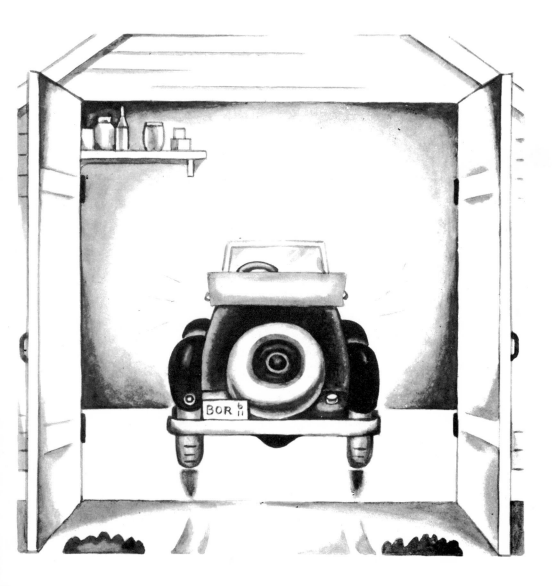

and
that's all!

# *The*
# LITTLE
# SAIL BOAT
## *By* LOIS LENSKI

## HENRY Z. WALCK, INC.
### NEW YORK

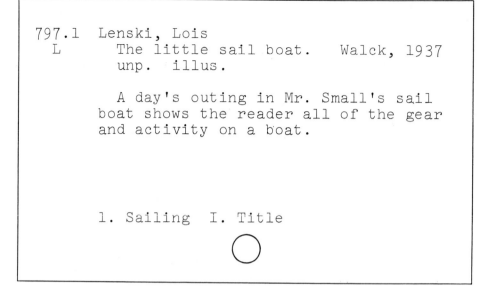

797.1  Lenski, Lois
   L      The little sail boat.   Walck, 1937
          unp.  illus.

          A day's outing in Mr. Small's sail
          boat shows the reader all of the gear
          and activity on a boat.


          1. Sailing  I. Title

This Main Entry catalog card may be reproduced without permission

The Little Sail-Boat

Captain Small has a
sail-boat. He keeps it
anchored off-shore.

It is a fine day. Captain Small gets into his row-boat and rows out. He is taking his fishing-line, lunch basket and small dog, Tinker, with him.

Captain Small takes
in the oars and makes
the row-boat fast to
the mooring.

He gets aboard
the sail-boat and hoists
the sail.

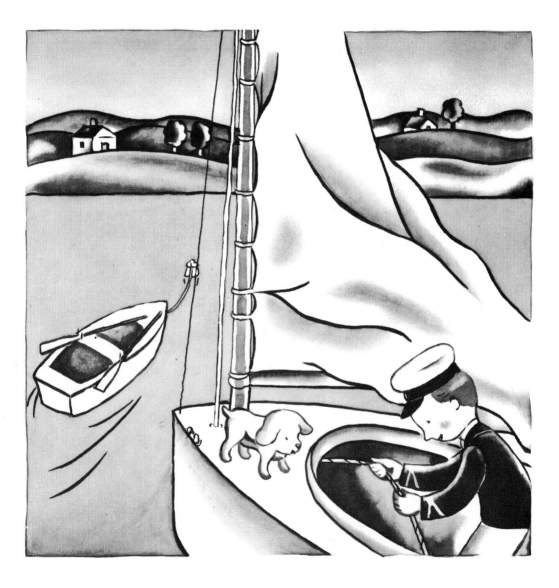

He drops the mooring and the boat starts to move. Tinker sits in the bow. He likes to sail, too.

Sitting in the stern,
Captain Small takes the
tiller and puts the boat
before the wind. He sails
for some distance.

He decides to jibe — to turn toward the shore. He pulls the tiller and ducks his head to let the sail swing over to the other side.

Now he is sitting with his back to the wind,- or, to windward.

He comes into a quiet little cove where the fishing is good.    He drops the anchor and lowers sail.

Captain Small gets out
his fishing-line and puts
bait on the hook. He throws
it away from the boat; the
cork floats on the water.
Now he is waiting for a
nibble!

He waits...and waits... but all the fish seem to be somewhere else. The sun is hot...and Captain Small grows tired of waiting. He falls asleep...

Suddenly a sharp tug on the line wakes him up. He pulls it in and finds a big, fat fish wiggling on the hook. He is so excited that...

He tumbles overboard!
Tinker barks! But never
mind! The water is so
nice and cool, he decides
to enjoy a good swim.

When he climbs back on deck, he feels very hungry, so he and Tinker eat their lunch. The sun soon dries his clothes.

Captain Small rests
awhile and then it is time
to start for home.    He
hoists the sail and raises
anchor.

On the way back, he
sails against the wind
in a zigzag course.

A speed-boat roars by.
The waves rock the sail-
boat and make the sails
flap. Tinker does not like it.

The sky grows dark. The waves splash over the bow. The wind blows hard. The boat heels over and almost upsets. But brave Captain Small brings it up into the wind. Then he sails safely into the bay.

Captain Small makes the sail-boat fast to the mooring. He and Tinker get into the row-boat. He rows as fast as he can to the dock.

Just as they climb out,
the downpour comes. They
are waiting in the boat-
house until it is over.

After the storm,
Captain Small and Tinker
drive home in
      the little Auto!

That night, Captain Small
has fish for supper. Tinker
has two dog biscuits.
Are they good?

Oh my!

Yes,
that's all!

# The
# LITTLE
# AIRPLANE

## By LOIS LENSKI

HENRY Z. WALCK, INC.

629.13  Lenski, Lois
   L          The little airplane.    Walck, 1938
             unp. · illus.

             Simply and accurately presented
           story of Mr. Small and his airplane.
           Gives information about how an air-
           plane flies and what its basic parts
           are.



             1. Airplanes        I. Title

Copyright 1938 Lois Lenski. Copyright © renewed 1966 by Lois Lenski.
All rights reserved. ISBN: 0-8098-1004-2. Library of Congress Catalog
Card Number: 59-12487. Printed in the United States of America.

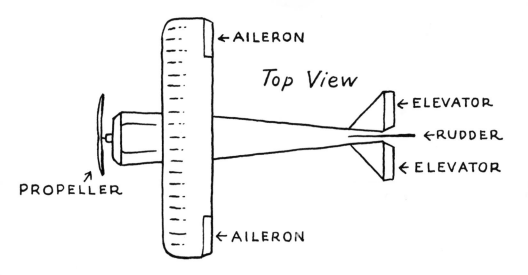

←AILERON

*Top View*

←ELEVATOR

←RUDDER

←ELEVATOR

PROPELLER

←AILERON

The Little Airplane

Pilot Small has a little airplane. He keeps it in the hangar at the airport.

It is a fine, sunny day. Pilot Small and the mechanic roll the airplane out of the hangar. Pilot Small decides to go up. They look the motor over carefully. They fill the tanks with gas.

All is ready for the take-off. Pilot Small climbs into the cockpit and sits down. He fastens his safety belt. He looks round on all sides to make sure the field is clear.

Pilot Small pumps the throttle a few times to prime the engine. The mechanic winds the propeller until the gas gets into the motor. Then he calls, "Contact!" Pilot Small turns on the switch and answers, "Contact!" The mechanic pulls the propeller through and it starts whizzing. The engine starts with a loud roar.

Pilot Small races the engine a few times. It roars loudly. He releases the brake. He looks at the wind indicator to see which way the wind is blowing. He taxies to the end of the field, in order to bring the plane round into the wind. He keeps the stick back to raise the elevators. The wind pressure on them keeps the plane down.

Now he is ready to take off. The motor is warmed up. He allows the stick to go forward gradually, until the tail-skid lifts. When flying speed is reached, he pulls back gently on the stick. This raises the elevators and lifts the plane off the ground. The plane climbs steeply into the wind.

The little airplane rises in the air. Pilot Small looks down and watches the ground slip away beneath him. He keeps one hand on the gas.

Up and up the little airplane goes until it reaches a height of 2000 feet. Pilot Small pushes the stick half-way forward, into neutral, to level off. The plane flies along smoothly.

Pilot Small decides to make a right turn. He pushes the stick to the right. This lowers the aileron on the left wing and raises the aileron on the right wing. At the same time, he presses on the rudder bar with his right foot, turning the rudder to the right. The plane *banks* as it turns to the right. Then he straightens the rudder and puts the stick back to neutral, to come out of the turn. He continues on a straight course.

The little airplane flies over a large lake. It hits the air pocket and drops thirty feet. The jolt gives Pilot Small an empty feeling in his stomach, but he does not mind. He flies low over the lake. He peeps out and sees his little Sail Boat rocking at anchor beneath him. He speeds up his motor and the little airplane climbs again.

The little airplane flies over a town. Pilot Small sees the people walking about like little ants on the streets below.

The little airplane climbs higher and higher. It climbs up through open holes in the clouds toward the blue sky above. It flies above the clouds. Pilot Small likes this the best of all! He sees the clouds like layers and layers of cotton beneath him. It is a very beautiful sight!

The little airplane glides down through the clouds. It sinks gently through the foggy, dry mist. Now it is below the clouds. Pilot Small sees the ground appear again beneath him.

Pilot Small decides to do a loop. He pushes the throttle wide open to gain speed. He puts the stick forward to put the nose down. He pulls back on the stick gradually. The little airplane dives first, then climbs up sharply, turns over and comes back to its first position. Pilot Small is pushed down into his seat. He gasps for breath, then gives a chuckle. He feels very proud of himself. He does another loop just for fun!

Just then the engine begins to sputter. Chuck-a, chuck-a, chuck-a-a - - It stops dead. The gas line is clogged. The little airplane glides and begins to sink slowly. Pilot Small looks worried.

Pilot Small looks for a safe landing place. He sees an open field at the edge of a dense forest. Perhaps it is a swamp. Perhaps it is full of rocks and stones. He hopes not for he will have to make a forced landing.

The little airplane glides to the ground. It lands safely in a grassy field. Pilot Small climbs out of the cockpit. He takes tools from his tool box. He fixes the gas line and his motor begins to hum once more. What a relief! Pilot Small smiles broadly. He takes off again. Away goes the little airplane!

It is growing late. Pilot Small banks again to return. He flies back to the airport. He flies low over his home. He sees his fields, his house and his garage. Circling above the airport, he sees his little Auto waiting for him beside the hangar.

The flight is over. Pilot Small decides to land. He circles to the right of the field. He looks at the wind indicator to see which way the wind is blowing. He decides on a point on the field which he wishes to hit and keeps his eye on it. He throttles his motor down to lose speed. He glides down against the wind.

As he comes close to the ground, he pulls the stick back to level off. The little airplane drops to the ground. It makes a perfect three-point landing. The two wheels and the tail-skid hit the ground at the same moment.

Pilot Small sets one brake and turns round. He taxies, *bumpety-bump*, to the hangar. He shuts off the motor. The propeller stops. He opens the door of the cockpit and steps out.

Pilot Small and the mechanic roll the little airplane into the hangar. Pilot Small jumps into his little Auto and drives off!

And that's all

about Pilot Small!